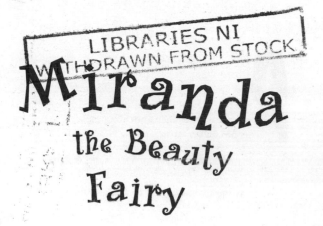

Miranda
the Beauty
Fairy

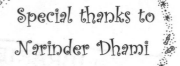

Special thanks to
Narinder Dhami

ORCHARD BOOKS
338 Euston Road, London NW1 3BH
Orchard Books Australia
Level 17/207 Kent Street, Sydney, NSW 2000
A Paperback Original

First published in 2012 by Orchard Books

HiT entertainment

A CIP catalogue record for this book is available
from the British Library.

ISBN 978 1 40831 674 0

1 3 5 7 9 10 8 6 4 2

Printed in Great Britain

The paper and board used in this paperback are natural recyclable
products made from wood grown in sustainable forests. The
manufacturing processes conform to the environmental regulations
of the country of origin.

Orchard Books is a division of Hachette Children's Books,
an Hachette UK company

www.hachette.co.uk

Miranda
the Beauty
Fairy

by Daisy Meadows

ORCHARD

www.rainbowmagic.co.uk

Jack Frost's Spell

I'm the king of designer fashion,
Looking stylish is my passion.
Ice Blue's the name of my fashion range,
Some people think my clothes are strange.

Do I care, though? Not a bit!
My designer label will be a hit.
The Fashion Fairies' magic will make that come true:
Soon everyone will wear Ice Blue!

Contents

A Splash of Magic   9

The Fashion Fairies   25

Ice Blue   35

Makeover Mayhem   45

Pondweed Perfume!   55

Miranda's Magic Bubbles   67

A Splash of Magic

"This is amazing, Rachel!"

Her eyes wide, Kirsty Tate stared up at the enormous glittering steel and glass building in front of them. Across the entrance was a sign reading *Tippington Fountains Shopping Centre*.

"Yes, isn't it?" Rachel Walker agreed. "I'm so glad you're staying with me for half-term so that you could be here for the grand opening, Kirsty."

"Me, too," Kirsty said eagerly. "And I'm *really* looking forward to seeing Jessica Jarvis!" The famous supermodel was the star guest at the new shopping centre's opening ceremony. Crowds of people had already gathered, waiting for the ceremony to begin.

"I think we're just in time for the parade," Mrs Walker said, locking her car. "Come along, girls."

Rachel, Kirsty and Mrs Walker hurried to join the crowd. Moments later the first float appeared around the side of the building.

"Every shop in the mall has its own float, Kirsty," Rachel explained. "Look, the first one is *Tippington Toys.*"

The float rumbled slowly towards them. A huge inflatable teddy bear sat on the

back of the truck. Also on the float were
two girls dressed as rag dolls with yellow
wool pigtails and flouncy dresses, and a
boy wearing a red soldier uniform. They
waved to the crowds as they passed by.

"The next one is *The Book Nook*,"
Kirsty said, reading the painted banner
strung across the float.

The Book Nook's float carried people
dressed as characters from storybooks.

The girls spotted Snow White, Cinderella and Pinocchio. This was followed by the *Sweet Scoop Ice Cream Parlour* float with its giant foam ice cream cones and ice lollies.

"Those ice creams look lovely!" Kirsty laughed.

Rachel sniffed the air. "I can *smell* something lovely, too," she said.

"So can I," Kirsty replied as delicious scents wafted past her nose. "Strawberries and vanilla!"

"The *Bath Bliss* float is coming," Mrs Walker said.

"They sell hair and body products."

A banner flying across the float proclaimed *"We only use natural organic ingredients!"* Rachel and Kirsty laughed when they saw that the float was loaded with bubble machines spraying hundreds of shimmering, scented bubbles into the crowds.

"Magical!" Rachel sighed. She caught a strawberry-scented bubble on her finger before it popped gently. "They look like fairy bubbles, Kirsty!"

The girls exchanged a quick smile. Their friendship

with the fairies was a *very* special secret.

"Look, girls, here's the last float," Mrs Walker said a little while later. "And can you see who's on it?"

"Jessica Jarvis!" Rachel and Kirsty chorused excitedly.

Jessica sat on a plush golden throne, waving to the crowds. She wore a sapphire-coloured dress, and her long blonde hair was piled elegantly on top of her head.

"Isn't she pretty?" Kirsty murmured.

Everyone cheered as the float stopped outside the doors

of the shopping centre. A small platform with a microphone had been set up, and a group of local councillors, including the mayor in her robes and chain, were waiting. Rachel and Kirsty could see a red ribbon tied across the doors.

Jessica Jarvis was helped down from the float and onto the stage to thunderous applause.

"Good morning, everyone," Jessica said, smiling. "I'm so pleased to be here to open this wonderful new shopping centre, *Tippington Fountains*. But before I do, I have a very special announcement to make…"

Rachel and Kirsty listened eagerly.

"The owners of the shopping centre have asked me to launch a brand-new children's competition," Jessica went on. "We want you to design and make your own outfits! They'll be judged in two days' time, and the winners will be modelling them in a charity fashion show at the end of this week."

There was more applause.

"And the Design-and-Make Competition *isn't* about looking like a model," Jessica added. "It's all about using your imagination and coming up with a unique outfit."

"Shall we enter, Kirsty?" Rachel said.

"Definitely!" Kirsty agreed.

The mayor handed Jessica a large pair

of scissors.

"And now…"
Jessica said, "I
know you're
longing to see
all the lovely
new shops.
So I declare
this shopping
centre open!"
And with a
flourish, she cut the
red ribbon in half.

There was more applause as the glass
doors swung open. Then the girls and
Mrs Walker followed the rest of the
crowd into the mall.

"It's just as amazing inside as outside!"
Kirsty declared, staring around in

wonderment. Glitter-ball lights and
enormous hanging baskets holding lush
green ferns were suspended from the
tall glass ceilings, and the floors were
decorated with swirling patterns of silver
mosaic tiles. Kirsty could hardly believe
how many different shops there were,
all with wonderful window displays.

"The fountains in the middle of the mall are supposed to be spectacular, too," said Mrs Walker.

"Oh, can we see them?" Rachel asked.

"You and Kirsty go, and I'll meet you back here in half an hour," Mrs Walker suggested. "One of the shops is offering free makeovers." She pointed to a nearby  cosmetics shop, *Beautiful You*. "I thought I'd try a new look for the party we're going to this weekend."

Rachel grinned. "Great idea, Mum. That'll give Dad a surprise!"

Mrs Walker laughed. "See you later,

girls," she said.

The girls were walking through the shopping centre when suddenly Kirsty gave Rachel a nudge.

"Look!" Kirsty whispered. "It's Jessica Jarvis!"

Jessica was standing next to the press office booth. A woman was interviewing her while a photographer snapped pictures.

"They're probably from the local paper," Rachel guessed. "Oh, look, Kirsty – the fountains!"

The girls had reached the centre of the mall and, as Mrs Walker had said, the fountains were spectacular.

The central fountain was in the middle of a large, clear blue pool, and its sparkling jet of water shot up almost as high as the mall roof. Around the big fountain was a circle of smaller fountains that sprayed water at random every so often. There

was a cascading waterfall at one end
of the pool, and the whole area was
surrounded by huge pots of tropical
flowers in vivid shades of scarlet and
orange.

"It's gorgeous!"
Kirsty exclaimed
as she and
Rachel
paused by
the edge of
the pool.

Suddenly
the small
fountain nearest
to them sent out
a spray of water. The
girls jumped in surprise as they felt a few
drops splash their faces.

Then Kirsty glanced up and noticed a tiny, intensely bright sparkle on top of the fountain.

"Rachel," she whispered, pointing upwards. "Look! What's that?"

"I'm not sure," Rachel whispered back. "Could it be – *a fairy*?"

The Fashion Fairies

As Rachel and Kirsty watched, the
sparkle swirled down from the top of the
fountain. It floated towards one of the
pots and landed on a scarlet, trumpet-
shaped flower. Now the excited girls
could see that the sparkle really *was* a
tiny fairy.

"Kirsty, it's Phoebe the Fashion Fairy!"

Rachel gasped as she recognised their old friend.

Phoebe stood on tiptoe on top of the flower and waved her wand in greeting.

"Hello, girls," she called in her lilting voice. "It's wonderful to see you again."

"Hello, Phoebe!" Kirsty beamed at her. "How are you, and how are all the other Party Fairies?"

"Everyone in Fairyland is fine, and they're all hoping to see you very soon," Phoebe replied, her eyes twinkling. "That's why I'm here, to invite you to come back to Fairyland with me!"

Rachel and Kirsty looked thrilled.

"A big fashion show is taking place in the grand hall of the Fairyland Palace," Phoebe went on. "It's been organised by my seven helpers, the Fashion Fairies. Would you like to come?"

"Yes, please!" Kirsty and Rachel said together, sounding so eager that Phoebe laughed. She flitted out of sight behind the fountain, and the girls rushed to join her. With one wave of Phoebe's wand, a cloud of glittering fairy magic surrounded Rachel and Kirsty, turned them into fairies, and carried them gently away to Fairyland.

Just a few seconds later Phoebe, Rachel and Kirsty arrived in the grand hall of the royal palace. King Oberon and Queen Titania were seated on their golden thrones, and the other fairies were sitting around a long catwalk, waiting for the fashion show to begin.

"Phoebe's brought Kirsty and Rachel!" called Amber the Orange Fairy, and there were whoops of delight.

"Welcome, girls!" said Pearl the Cloud Fairy.

"We're so glad you could join us," India the Moonstone Fairy added.

Phoebe escorted a smiling Rachel and Kirsty over to the king and queen.

"Girls, we're thrilled to have you with us once again!" King Oberon declared.

"The Fashion Fairies always put on a fabulous show," Queen Titania told them. "Phoebe, why don't you introduce Rachel and Kirsty to your helpers?"

Phoebe nodded. She led the girls over to the front row of the audience where seven fairies were seated.

"Girls, meet Miranda the Beauty Fairy,
Claudia the Accessories Fairy, Tyra the
Dress Designer Fairy, Alexa the Fashion
Reporter Fairy, Matilda the Hair Stylist
Fairy, Brooke the Photographer Fairy
and Lola the Fashion Show Fairy,"
Phoebe said, pointing her wand at each
fairy in turn.

"Hello, girls!" the Fashion Fairies
called. Rachel and Kirsty could see
that each fairy had an object that
shimmered with magic. Miranda held
a lipstick in a gold case, Claudia wore
a long necklace hung with charms,
Tyra had a tape measure, Alexa a pen,
Matilda a hairbrush and Brooke a
camera. The seventh fairy, Lola, had
a special backstage pass on a ribbon
around her neck.

"We look after all kinds of fashion in both the human and the fairy worlds with the help of our magical objects," Miranda the Beauty Fairy explained. She was a slender fairy with light brown hair, dressed in cropped jeans, a pink top and a blue jacket with a furry collar.

Suddenly there was a fanfare of trumpets and Bertram the frog footman stepped out from behind the magnificent velvet curtains.

"It's time for the fashion
show to begin!" he
announced with a bow.

Rachel and Kirsty
hurried to take their
places next to the king
and queen. Meanwhile
Phoebe stepped up
onto the catwalk.

"Our very first model is Ruby the Red
Fairy," Phoebe announced. Rachel and
Kirsty clapped loudly. Ruby was their
oldest friend, the very first fairy they'd
met on their holiday to Rainspell Island.

There was a round of applause as
Ruby stepped out from behind the
curtains. She looked beautiful in a red
silk dress, the full skirt swirling around
her ankles.

Rachel and Kirsty watched as Ruby walked to the end of the catwalk and twirled. But right at that moment a freezing ice bolt zoomed over the heads of the audience from the back of the hall. The girls clapped their hands to their mouths in horror as the ice bolt crashed onto the catwalk. Ruby gave a little scream. Then, to everyone's amazement, her dress turned from a beautiful red to an icy-blue colour.

"What's happening?" Rachel gasped. "Ruby's dress has changed colour, and look! A picture has appeared on her skirt!"

Kirsty peered at the picture. "I don't believe it!" she said shakily. "Rachel, it's a picture of *Jack Frost!*"

Ice
Blue

Rachel, Kirsty and the fairies watched in
shock as Ruby stared down at her dress
in disbelief. Suddenly Jack Frost himself
appeared at the back of the hall, riding
on an ice bolt. He hurtled towards the
catwalk, a smug grin on his frosty face.
He was followed by a gaggle of goblins.

"What's Jack Frost up to?" Kirsty whispered to Rachel as he jumped off the ice bolt onto the catwalk.

"And what's he *wearing*?" Rachel murmured, hardly able to believe her eyes.

Jack Frost was dressed in an ice-blue jacket with enormous shoulder pads. He wore clunky, unlaced boots and tight leggings with a star pattern. The goblins were also wearing strange, mismatched outfits. One wore a top hat and a pair of blue shorts, while another sported a blue dinner jacket with a bow tie and a blue T-shirt.

"Clear the catwalk!" Jack Frost shouted, glaring at Ruby and Phoebe. "The style king is here!"

The goblins applauded as Jack Frost

paraded up and down the catwalk.

"Our fantastic outfits are from a stylish new fashion label called Ice Blue," Jack Frost went on. "And guess what? All the clothes are designed by ME!"

"But *you're* not a fashion designer, Jack Frost!" Tyra the Dress Designer Fairy said, in horror.

Jack Frost shot her an icy glare. "We'll see about that!" he declared. "I know all about fashion, and I'm so handsome, I want *everyone* to look like me." He strutted along the catwalk, preening himself. "Soon every single human and all you fairies will ONLY be wearing clothes by Ice Blue. Just think how stylish everyone will be!"

Rachel and Kirsty glanced at each other in dismay as the goblins went wild. Then Queen Titania stood up.

"This is all very silly, Jack Frost," the queen said sternly. "But you're welcome to stay and watch our fashion show if you'll turn Ruby's dress red again."

"I don't think so!" Jack Frost sneered. Raising his wand, he sent an ice bolt whizzing straight towards Queen Titania. Bertram sprang up to defend her, but he couldn't stop Jack Frost's spell. The queen's golden crown vanished and was replaced by a blue woolly hat with a huge pom-pom on top of it.

"How dare you, Jack Frost!" scolded
King Oberon, looking very upset. He
jumped to his feet as Bertram helped the
queen remove the silly
hat. "You've gone too
far this time."

"And I'm not
finished yet!"
Jack Frost cackled
rudely. He pointed
his ice wand at the
seven Fashion Fairies
in the front row. Instantly, a
flurry of ice bolts zoomed towards them.
Rachel and Kirsty watched helplessly as
Jack Frost's magic swept all the Fashion
Fairies' magical objects away from them,
even lifting Claudia's necklace and Lola's
backstage pass over their heads.

The goblins roared with laughter as the objects flew across the catwalk and into Jack Frost's enormous pockets.

"And now I have all the Fashion Fairies' magic, I'm off to Tippington to win the charity fashion show!" Jack Frost announced. "Then very soon everyone, everywhere will be wearing my beautiful Ice Blue clothes!"

"Wait!" King Oberon shouted.

But Jack Frost waved his wand, and he
and his goblins disappeared in an icy-
blue mist.

"This is terrible!" Miranda the Beauty
Fairy said sadly. "Our fashion show is
ruined!"

"Nothing will go right now," Lola the
Fashion Show Fairy agreed, biting her
lip.

"That means the charity fashion show
will be a disaster, too," Claudia the
Accessories Fairy pointed out. "In fact,
fashion everywhere will be ruined unless
we get our magical objects back!"

"Rachel and I can help!" Kirsty said,
her eyes shining with determination.

"We'll do our best to find *all* the
magical objects," Rachel promised.

"Girls, you've come to our rescue once again," Queen Titania said gratefully. "Thank you for being such loyal friends." "Miranda the Beauty Fairy will return to *Tippington Fountains* with you," King Oberon told Rachel and Kirsty. "Good luck with your search."

"Good luck!" the fairies cried. Miranda waved her wand and the girls became human-size. With another flick of Miranda's wand, the three of them vanished in a cloud of fairy magic.

Makeover Mayhem

"It's time to meet my mum at *Beautiful You*," Rachel said as they arrived back at the fountains. "We can look for Miranda's magic lipstick on the way."

Miranda nodded and hid inside Kirsty's denim shoulder bag.

Quickly the girls retraced their steps through the mall. There were lots of people around, and Rachel wondered how on earth they would spot the

missing lipstick amongst the crowds.
But then she remembered what Queen
Titania always said. *Let the magic come
to you...*

The *Beautiful You* shop was very busy.
Through the windows Rachel and Kirsty
could see lots of women sitting on stools
at the counters, having makeovers.

"There's my mum," Rachel said,
spotting the back of her mother's head. A
girl in a white overall
was applying
blusher to Mrs
Walker's cheeks
with a large
fluffy brush.

Rachel and
Kirsty went into
the shop, Miranda

keeping well out of sight. *Beautiful You*
was filled with shelves of all kinds of
make-up in every colour imaginable.
The girls looked particularly hard at the
lipsticks as they passed by, but none of
them shimmered with fairy magic.

"Hi, Mum," said Rachel, tapping Mrs
Walker on the shoulder.

Rachel's mum turned around, and
the girls gasped in shock. Mrs Walker's
face was caked in thick, gaudy
make-up. Her eye shadow
was emerald green, her
mascara was bright
blue and she had two
circles of crimson
blusher, one on each
cheek. She looked like
a circus clown.

"What's the matter?" Mrs Walker asked, turning around to look in the mirror. She stared at herself in complete horror. "Oh, my goodness! I look awful!"

"I'm *so* sorry," the girl in the white overall mumbled in an embarrassed

voice. "I don't know what's wrong with me today."

The girls glanced around the room. Rachel's mum wasn't the only woman having a terrible makeover. There were plenty of other glum-looking customers who were also caked in heavy and unflattering make-up.

"This is all because my magical lipstick is missing!" Miranda whispered from Kirsty's bag. "All make-up looks horrible, and everyone has lost the smile that makes them naturally beautiful."

"Maybe we can help you fix it, Mum," Rachel suggested, but Mrs Walker shook her head gloomily.

"I'm going to the ladies' toilets to wipe it all off," she said, sliding off her stool. "Why don't you girls meet me at the *Sweet Scoop Ice Cream Parlour* in twenty minutes?"

"OK, Mum," Rachel replied.

"Maybe we should have a closer look around this shop before we go," Kirsty whispered to Rachel as Mrs

Walker left. "It's just the place to hide a magic lipstick! No one would notice it here."

Rachel and Kirsty began to wander quietly around *Beautiful You*, keeping their eyes open for Miranda's magical object. A few moments later, Rachel

noticed three women sitting in a corner.
They all had long flowing hair and they
were doing makeovers on each other,
applying lipstick and patting on face
powder. Rachel could see that two of the
women looked just as glum and badly
made-up as her mum and the other
customers. But to her surprise the third
woman didn't look the same at all! *Her*

make-up was beautifully applied, and she was smiling happily.

"Isn't that odd, Kirsty?" Rachel murmured, pointing the woman out to her friend. "How come *her* make-up looks so good?"

Kirsty was about to reply when she suddenly noticed the clothes the three women were wearing. All of them were dressed in ice-blue outfits exactly the same colour as Jack Frost's jacket.

"Rachel, they're goblins!" Kirsty whispered. "Look at their clothes!

They must be wearing wigs, and the face powder is hiding their green skin."

"And that smiling one whose make-up is so perfect has my lipstick!" Miranda realised. "Jack Frost must have given it to the goblins to hide."

"And they've got distracted, messing about with all this make-up!" Rachel guessed. "So, how are we going to get the lipstick back?"

Pondweed Perfume!

Before the girls and Miranda could
decide on a plan, the three goblins got up
and left the shop.

"I'll turn you into fairies," Miranda
decided. "It'll be much easier to follow
the goblins then. Otherwise we might lose
them in the crowds."

Rachel and Kirsty quickly ducked down behind the nearest make-up counter. With just one flick of Miranda's wand, the girls began to shrink. They became smaller and smaller until they were fairy-size, with fluttery wings like Miranda's on their shoulders.

Miranda beckoned to the girls. They flew silently from behind the make-up counter and out of the shop.

At once they spotted the goblins staring greedily into the window of a chocolate shop, pressing their noses against the glass. Miranda and the girls flew towards them, keeping out of sight by flitting behind the pillars and banners. But then the goblins moved off once again.

"Have you noticed all the shoppers look just as miserable as the people in *Beautiful You?*" Kirsty asked, frowning. "We *must* get Miranda's lipstick back – and all the other magical objects!"

The goblins had now reached the fountains in the middle of the mall. They squealed with delight and stopped to admire their reflections in the clear blue pool.

"This could be our chance!" Miranda decided.

Kirsty was sniffing the air. "What *is* that horrible smell?" she asked, wrinkling her nose and pulling a face.

"It smells like pondweed!" Rachel said. "Where's it coming from?"

Miranda pointed at the *Bath Bliss* shop on the other side of the pool. "All of *Bath Bliss's* products smell horrid because my lipstick is missing!" she explained.

Kirsty could see that the shoppers walking past *Bath Bliss* were holding their noses in disgust. "The goblins don't seem to mind," she remarked, gazing down at them. They were still staring at their reflections in the water.

"Oh, goblins love bad smells!" Miranda told her.

Just then, Rachel spotted a big sign in

the *Bath Bliss* window.

"*Try our beautiful bubbles for free!*" she read aloud. "*We're giving away a free trial bottle of our chocolate and orange scented bubble bath, while stocks last.*" There was a big stack of bubble-bath bottles next to the sign.

Rachel's face lit up. "Oh, that's given me an idea!" she exclaimed. "But I need to be human-size again, Miranda."

The three of them flew to hide behind another pillar, and Miranda's magic quickly restored Rachel to her normal size. Immediately, Rachel hurried off to *Bath Bliss* while Kirsty and Miranda fluttered over to the pot of tropical flowers nearest to the three goblins. There they slipped inside one of the large scarlet blooms to hide.

The horrible smell got much stronger as Rachel went inside *Bath Bliss*, so she wasn't surprised to find the shop empty.

The girl sitting behind the counter was looking very miserable.

"Hello, can I help you?" she asked.

"Could I try one of your free bottles of bubble bath?" Rachel asked, pointing at the window display.

"Are you sure?" the girl asked with a sigh. "I don't know what's wrong with this batch, but something's gone wrong because they smell really bad!"

"I'd really like one," Rachel assured her.
So the shop assistant took a bottle out of
the window and handed it over. Rachel
thanked her and then hurried back to the
fountains. To her relief, the three goblins
were still there.

"Oh, hello!"
Rachel said.
"I just had to
come over and
tell you that
I think you
all look very
beautiful."

The goblins
smiled smugly.
"We already
know that!" said the
one with the perfect make-up.

"Maybe one day *you'll* be as beautiful as us, if you try hard enough!" one of the others told Rachel, and all three goblins roared with laughter.

Meanwhile, Kirsty and Miranda were peeping out of the tropical flower, watching what was going on.

"Wouldn't you like to *smell* beautiful, too?" Rachel asked, holding out the bottle of bubble bath. "Maybe you'd like to share this between you."

The third goblin grabbed the bubble bath, twisted the cap off and smelt it. "Ooh, it's *lovely!*" he sighed. "I'm keeping it all for myself."

"I'm the most beautiful, so I should have it!" the goblin with the perfect make-up insisted. He made a grab for the bottle, but the other goblin held it high above his head, out of his reach. Rachel smiled as the third goblin sneaked up behind the second goblin, jumped up high and snatched the bottle. Laughing triumphantly, he waved it in the air.

"Give me that!" shouted the goblin with the perfect make-up. He lunged

at the bottle, and all three goblins began tussling over it. The top of the bottle flew off as they did so.

Rachel waited quietly as Miranda and Kirsty flew out of the scarlet flower. They circled the goblins, trying to spot the lipstick, and Kirsty managed to slip her hand into the perfectly made-up goblin's pocket. To her dismay, it was empty, and she didn't have time to search his other pocket. Quickly she and

Miranda fluttered behind one of the pots
of flowers again before they were spotted.

Suddenly there was a splash as the
bottle slipped through the goblin's fingers
and fell into the pool.

"Now look what you've done, you
idiot!" the goblins all shouted at each
other.

The water began frothing up into big,
soapy bubbles. Rachel pulled a face as
the smell of pondweed grew stronger, too.

"Oh, that smell's getting worse!" a
passing shopper remarked to her friend.

"Lovely perfume!" sighed one of the
goblins happily, and he flicked some of
the bubbles at the others.

And that was when an idea popped
into Kirsty's head!

Miranda's Magic Bubbles

"Miranda, could you magic up *loads* more stinky bubbles to distract the goblins?" Kirsty whispered.

"Of course!" Miranda replied, surprised. She pointed her wand at the fountain pool and a few magical sparkles landed on the surface of the water. Immediately, the water began to foam and froth. Hundreds of bubbles appeared and floated up into the air, drifting around the goblins. The smell of pondweed was now so overpowering that the shoppers nearby ran for cover, and Rachel covered her nose with both hands.

"Bubbles!" shrieked the goblins with delight. "Lovely, stinky bubbles!" They began scooping up armfuls of bubbles and throwing them at each other.

Kirsty beckoned to Miranda. They both took a deep breath, held their noses and whizzed out from behind the pot of flowers, watching the goblins for any sign of Miranda's magical lipstick.

The goblins were running around the fountain pool, enjoying their bubble fight and getting quite wet. Suddenly, Kirsty saw something golden fall out of the beautifully made-up goblin's other pocket and roll across the floor of the mall. It was the magic lipstick! But the goblin

was having so
much fun, he
didn't notice.

Kirsty and
Miranda
flew towards
it as fast as
they could.
As soon
as Miranda
touched the
lipstick, it immediately shrank down to
its Fairyland size. Miranda picked it up,
beaming at Kirsty, and Rachel clapped
her hands with delight.

In an instant the stink of pondweed
vanished and was replaced with the rich
scent of chocolate and oranges.

"Yuck!" the made-up goblin shouted,

pulling a face. Rachel noticed that his beautiful make-up had now vanished completely. "What's that *horrible* smell?"

"Let's get out of here!" another yelled. Holding their noses, they scurried off through the mall.

The shoppers began to return, and Rachel hurried to join Kirsty and Miranda who were hiding behind one of the small fountains.

"Look, everyone's smiling again, and there are lots of customers going into the *Bath Bliss* shop!" Rachel pointed out.

"*And* everyone's crazy make-up is much more natural now," Kirsty added as she saw some of the customers from *Beautiful You* walking past.

"I'm smiling, too!" Miranda said with a big grin. "Thank you so much, girls. You've done it again! Everyone in Fairyland will be thrilled when I return with *this*!" And she held up her lipstick. "But you will keep looking for the other magical objects, won't you?"

"We promise!" the girls said.

Quickly Miranda's magic turned Kirsty

back to human-size. Then, waving her wand in farewell, Miranda disappeared in a puff of rainbow-coloured magic.

"Time to meet my mum at the *Sweet Scoop Ice Cream Parlour*," Rachel said, glancing up at a clock.

"I think we deserve a little celebration!" Kirsty laughed.

The girls hurried off.

"You know, I've been thinking about the Design-and-Make Competition," Kirsty remarked as they waited outside the ice cream parlour for Mrs Walker. "All those bright, tropical flowers around the fountain have given me some ideas!"

"I'd like to use lots of colours in my outfit, too," Rachel agreed. "Oh, here comes Mum – and she looks like herself again, thank goodness!"

Mrs Walker was coming towards them, smiling. To the girls' relief, her clown make-up had vanished, and she looked beautifully natural again.

"Everyone's happy now that Miranda's lipstick is back where it belongs," said Kirsty.

"But there are still six magical objects missing," Rachel reminded her. "I hope we find the next one very soon!"

Now it's time for Kirsty and
Rachel to help...

Claudia
the Accessories Fairy

Read on for a sneak peek...

"Here we are," Mr Walker said, parking
the car at *Tippington Fountains
Shopping Centre.* He glanced over to
where his daughter Rachel and her best
friend Kirsty Tate were sitting in the
back seat. "I know you only came here
yesterday, girls, but I need to pick up a
shirt. I'll be as quick as I can."

"Don't worry, Dad," Rachel said,
exchanging a secret smile with Kirsty as
they got out of the car. "We don't mind
at all. Take as long as you like!"

It was the second day of half-term, and
Kirsty was staying with Rachel's family.
Whenever the two friends got together,
magical things always seemed to happen
– and they certainly had yesterday!
Rachel's mum had brought the girls to
the shopping centre, as it was the grand
opening day, with lots of free activities
to take part in, and a whole procession
of colourful floats. It had all been really
fun and exciting…especially when the
girls had found themselves whisked off to
Fairyland, and thrown into a brand-new
fairy adventure. Hurrah!

"I hope we meet another fairy today,"
Kirsty whispered eagerly to Rachel, as
they made their way through the car
park to the lifts.

"Oh, me too," Rachel replied.
"Yesterday was amazing. But you know

what Queen Titania always says: we can't go looking for magic. We have to wait for it to come to us." She grinned. "I just hope it finds us again soon, that's all!"

The three of them went up in the lift. "Ground floor," a voice from the speaker announced after a few moments. "Welcome to *Tippington Fountains Shopping Centre!*"

Read **Claudia the Accessories Fairy** to find out what adventures are in store for Kirsty and Rachel!

Meet the
Fashion Fairies

If Kirsty and Rachel don't find the Fashion Fairies'
magical objects, Jack Frost will ruin fashion forever!

www.rainbowmagicbooks.co.uk

Meet the fairies, play games
and get sneak peeks at
the latest books!

www.rainbowmagicbooks.co.uk

There's fairy fun for everyone on
our wonderful website.
You'll find great activities, competitions, stories and
fairy profiles, and also a special newsletter.

Get 30% off all Rainbow Magic books at
www.rainbowmagicbooks.co.uk

Enter the code RAINBOW at the checkout.
Offer ends 31 December 2012.

Offer valid in United Kingdom and Republic of Ireland only.

Competition!

Here's a friend who Kirsty and Rachel met in an earlier story. Use the clues below to help you guess her name. When you have enjoyed all seven of the Fashion Fairies books, arrange the first letters of each mystery fairy's name to make a special word, then send us the answer!

CLUES

1. This special fairy has short blonde hair.

2. She wears a beautiful purple puffball skirt.

3. One of her magical items is a memory book.

The fairy's name is _ _ _ _ _ _ _ _ the _ _ _ _ _ _ _ _ _ Fairy

We will put all of the correct entries into a draw and select one winner to receive a special Fashion Fairies goody bag. Your name will also be featured in a forthcoming Rainbow Magic story!

Enter online now at www.rainbowmagicbooks.co.uk

No purchase required. Only one entry per child. Two prize draws will take place on 31 May 2013 and 31 August 2013. Alternatively readers can send the answers on a postcard to: Rainbow Magic Fashion Fairies Competition, Orchard Books, 338 Euston Road, London, NW1 3BH. Australian readers can write to: Rainbow Magic Fashion Fairies Competition, Hachette Children's Books, Level 17/207 Kent St, Sydney, NSW 2000. E-mail: childrens.books@hachette.com.au. New Zealand readers should write to: Rainbow Magic Fashion Fairies Competition, 4 Whetu Place, Mairangi Bay, Auckland, NZ

The Complete Book of Fairies

Packed with secret fairy facts
and extra-special rainbow reveals, this magical guide
includes all you need to know about your favourite
Rainbow Magic friends.

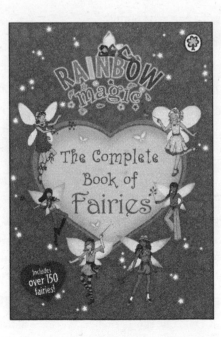

Out Now!